THE LEGEND OF ZELDA
ORACLE OF SEASONS

By Craig Wessel

Scholastic Inc.

New York   Toronto   London   Auckland   Sydney
Mexico City   New Delhi   Hong Kong   Buenos Aires

ISBN 0-439-36709-3

TM, ® and Game Boy Color are trademarks of Nintendo. © 2001 Nintendo.

All rights reserved. Published by Scholastic Inc.
SCHOLASTIC and associated logos are trademarks and/or regis-tered trademarks of Scholastic Inc.

12 11 10 9 8 7 6 5 4 3   1 2 3 4 5 6/0

Printed in the U.S.A.
First Scholastic printing, October 2001

The Legend of Zelda:
Oracle of Seasons

Since *The Legend of Zelda* was released for the original Nintendo Entertainment System® in 1987, the *Zelda* series has earned a reputation for delivering action-packed gameplay mixed with deep storylines and unforgettable characters.

In this game — *Oracle of Seasons* — Onox, General of Darkness, has kidnapped Din, the Oracle of Seasons, and the seasons in the land of Holodrum are in chaos. Link, the Hyrulian Hero, must travel across a massive world exploring dungeons, collecting items, battling enemies, and completing quests in order to defeat the evil Onox and return Holodrum to normal.

How to Use This Book

This special book is more than just one story about Link and his adventures in the land of Holodrum. You get to decide what happens every time you read this book!

Start by reading the Introduction. The Introduction begins the story and introduces you to the main characters — Link, Din, and the evil Onox. The next section of the book is titled "The Adventure Begins." At the bottom of this page, you'll see a question and some choices, and you'll have the chance to make your first choice.

Once you've made your decision, turn to the page shown under your choice to continue the story. For example, if you choose "Bipin and Blossom's Home," turn to page 60 and you'll read about what happens next. As you read through the book, you'll make other decisions until you reach one of the book's endings.

That's the best part — there are several endings to this book! Some are good, but some of them are bad. Every time you read it, you can make a different set of decisions and read a brand-new story.

One more thing before you turn the page — this book is based on the Game Boy® Color game *The Legend of Zelda: Oracle of Seasons*, so read carefully — you just might find some clues that will lead to secrets in the game! Good luck, and have fun adventuring with Link!

Introduction

One day in Hyrule, a strange force drew Link into Hyrule Castle, where he found the Triforce resting, glittering brilliantly as it awaited him.

"Link . . . Link . . . accept the quest of the Triforce!"

A beam of light caught Link, and suddenly he vanished! He passed out, and when he woke up, he found himself in a forest he had never seen before. The sound of music drew him to a small clearing, where he found a troop of performers practicing.

"Join us," they said. "We are a troop of traveling actors." Link noticed a beautiful young girl dancing in circles. When she noticed Link, she called to him.

"Welcome to Holodrum. I am Din, the dancer. Would you like to dance with me?" Not waiting for his answer, Din took Link by the hand and he reluctantly began to dance. Unfortunately, the dance didn't last long.

Suddenly the sky went dark, and thunder crashed. A voice boomed, "I've found you, Din! You can't deceive me by disguising yourself as a dancer. I am Onox, General of Darkness! Now reveal yourself, Oracle of Seasons!"

A great whirlwind dropped from the sky and drew near Din. Link, who didn't know what was going on, knew he had to help her. "Help me, Link!" cried Din. But the whirlwind blew Link back as he struggled against its fury, and Din was swept away by the wind.

Link couldn't have known what would happen, but strange things began to occur in the land. With the Oracle of Seasons imprisoned by Onox, the seasons fell into chaos and the land was deprived of nature's gifts. Life was slowly being drained from the land as Onox set in motion his plan to drain power from the land and create a world of total darkness.

Will Link be able to rescue Din and save the land from the General of Darkness? It's up to you! Choose wisely in the next section — the fate of Holodrum is in your hands.

Turn to page 20.

8 The Clock Shop

Link thought the small shop near the center of the village looked like a good place to start, so he opened the door and stepped inside. "Hail, stranger," said the shopkeeper inside. "Have you found it?"

"Found it? I'm afraid not. . . . What exactly are you looking for?" asked Link.

"Why, the Wooden Bird, of course! I'm going to build the largest cucco clock in all of Holodrum, but I need the bird. Have you seen it anywhere?"

"No, I haven't," said Link, "but I'll keep an eye out for it."

Since there wasn't much to see inside the shop, Link turned to go. Out of the corner of his eye, he saw a stairway near the shopkeeper. *I wonder what's down there,* he thought. *If I find the Wooden Bird, maybe I can return and explore a bit.*

With a nod to the shopkeeper, Link opened the door and stepped back outside into the cold.

Turn to page 86.

The Village Shop

Link walked around the village, and he found a small shop. When he tried to enter, he noticed a sign hanging from the door.

CLOSED. COME AGAIN!

Closed . . . too bad, thought Link. *I could have used some supplies. I'll come back later and see if they've returned.*

Link pulled his cloak tighter against the cold wind and left the shop behind.

Turn to page 86.

10 Margaret and Amy

Link explored much more of the crypt. He made it past crumbling floors, evil creatures, and tricky traps, until he finally reached a large open room. Just beyond this room, he found a chamber with two ghosts inside — the one he had defeated earlier and another one. Their names (when they had names) were Margaret and Amy.

"You must keep the torches in this room lit, Link, or we'll send you back to the dungeon entrance!" they threatened. With that, the two ghosts began circling the room, heading for the torches. Link didn't waste any time. He loaded his slingshot with Ember Seeds and waited.

As soon as one of the ghosts blew out a torch, Link fired an Ember Seed at it to relight it. He kept this up to keep the torches lit, and he also used his sword on the ghosts whenever they floated nearby.

Finally, realizing that they couldn't blow out all the torches, and injured by Link's sword, the two ghosts disappeared, leaving Link free to keep exploring.

Turn to page 70.

Sword and Shield Dungeon 11

The Maku Tree told Link that the Sword and Shield Dungeon was in Subrosia, near the ruins of the Temple of Seasons. When Link arrived at the Temple ruins, he found a warp that sent him to an area he hadn't been able to reach before. When he stepped through the warp, he found a small cave to the north.

A Subrosian was throwing items into a lava pit, and he asked Link if he would throw a bomb into the pit for him. Link wasn't sure why he agreed, but he did. The bomb exploded, triggering a massive lava eruption. The Temple shook, and lava burned away walls, revealing areas Link hadn't been able to reach before.

Link searched the area on both sides of the warp to see what had changed, and he found his way to the Sword and Shield Dungeon entrance.

Turn to page 91.

12 Hero's Cave:
The Wooden Sword

In the southern chamber, Link avoided the attacking spiders and approached the locked door on the east side of the room. The small key fit the lock and, with a click, the door opened.

Link stepped into the next room. The room was divided by a huge pit that left a small ledge connected by a narrow walkway on the north side of the room. This room was swarming with spiders and Gels, so Link had to move fast to explore the room.

On the north side of the room, just west of the pit, Link found a small metal plate in the floor. When he stepped on it, a section of the north wall on the other side of the pit slid open, revealing another chamber. Link quickly crossed the narrow walkway on the east side of the room and entered the chamber.

Inside the chamber, a large chest sat in the center of the room. Link approached it, and it opened at his touch. Nestled inside the chest was a Wooden Sword! Link picked it up, but before he could admire it, he found himself on the beach outside the cave with the sword.

The Octoroks on the beach were no match for Link's new weapon, and he wiped them out quickly. Link explored the ledge above the cave and he found a gap in the

cliff that was blocked by bushes. Using his new sword, he cut down the bushes and stepped through the gap.

Here he found a hole in the ground below that he could not reach before. Confident that he could handle any enemies he might find, Link tucked his sword into his belt and jumped into the hole.

Turn to page 90.

14 Sword and Shield:
The Ice Chamber

North of the room where he defeated Frypolar, Link entered a large, icy room. The floor of this room was completely covered in ice, making his footing very slippery. Link carefully explored the chamber and found something interesting.

There were three ice blocks, and three regular stone blocks in the room. There was also a niche in the east wall of the room that looked like it would hold all three ice blocks. After a few tries, Link was sure that he had to get all the ice blocks into that niche in the wall to get to the next room. The only problem was, once he pushed an ice block, it wouldn't stop until it hit something solid — a stone block or a wall.

Link thought hard about this puzzle, then went to work moving blocks around. Here's the solution he came up with:

- Push the west block south one space to rest against the row of stone blocks.
- Push this same ice block east and it will bump the ice block to the east.
- Push this same ice block north, and it will bump another ice block.

- Push the northern ice block west, where it will rest against another stone block.
- Push this ice block south to rest against the row of blocks.
- Push this ice block east and it will bump the ice block to the east.
- Now push this ice block north, and all three blocks will be in a north-to-south line.
- Push all the blocks to the east, into the niche in the wall.

Once Link had pushed the ice blocks into the niche, a stairway appeared on the north side of the room, and Link used it to leave the room.

Turn to page 73.

16 Sword and Shield:
Basement Dungeon

The basement dungeon was lit by the fiery glow of lava far below. Link climbed down the stairs, which ended in a ledge that overlooked the lava. Across the lava, he could see another ledge, but it was hard to see because there were fireballs circling it. The room was also full of Keese, so Link used his Boomerang to get rid of them first.

Link watched the fireballs, then timed a jump between them to reach the ledge. Once he was on the ledge, he saw another ledge and timed another jump to reach it. Having made the difficult crossing, Link climbed the stairs that led from the ledge back upstairs.

Turn to page 36.

The Maku Tree

As soon as Link had all the Essences, he went to the Maku Tree in Horon Village. With its powers fully restored, the Maku Tree was now able to give Link the huge Maku Seed that was in its branches. The magical seed was the only thing that would let Link pass through the Northern Peak to reach Onox's Castle.

Before he left to battle Onox, Link warped to the Sunken City and went to Maple's house, where he bought a Magic Potion to help him in the battle. Once he had the potion, he was ready to fight Onox.

Turn to page 92.

18 Subrosia

Link found himself in a dark, underground world. The first two people he saw were oddly dressed, covered from head to toe in robes. They thought the same thing about him, and were reluctant to talk.

"What land is this?" asked Link. The two looked at each other.

"Subrosia, of course. What land are you from?" asked one of them.

"It doesn't matter. I'm looking for a Temple — did one show up here lately?"

"Yes!" the other Subrosian said. "A few days ago it appeared out of nowhere. It's located on the east side of the village."

Link thanked the Subrosians and turned to the south. There were two sets of stairs to choose from, both of them going south. One was on the east, and the other on the west side of the landing. Although he knew the Temple was to the east, Link decided to take the west stairs first to make sure there was nothing else he needed to see here.

Turn to page 75.

The Explorer's Crypt:
Basement

Link carefully made his way into the basement of the Crypt. Near the bottom of the stairs, he found several huge statues surrounding the stairs. As he explored the room, he also found that he was locked in — the door in the south wall was locked, and there was no other way out of the room.

He had been in enough situations like this to realize that the statues were probably the key to getting out of this room. As he pushed each one of the statues, they began to glow. Suddenly, they attacked! Link slashed at them with his sword and quickly destroyed all but one of them. The final statue had not glowed when he touched it, so he took a closer look at it. Near the statue, he saw a place on the floor that looked different, so he pushed the statue until it was on that spot. The door to the south opened, allowing Link to leave the room.

Link found a set of stairs and took them down to a lower level, where he found a Dungeon Map. *This will show me where the enemies, chests, and items are in the dungeon,* thought Link.

Turn to page 29.

20 The Adventure Begins

When the whirlwind had passed and Din was gone, Link didn't know what to do. As he searched the clearing, he found Impa, the cook, who had been injured in the attack. Link asked her if she knew what was going on.

"I'm afraid I do, Link," she said. "You see, I'm not really a cook. I'm Princess Zelda's nurse, and she sent me here to escort the Oracle of Seasons back to Hyrule. Now that I'm hurt and Din is gone, I don't think I can make it." Impa gasped in pain and Link helped her sit down.

"Please, Link, will you rescue Din and complete the quest Zelda gave to me?"

Link, who was sworn to serve Zelda, didn't hesitate. "Yes, Impa. I will. But tell me, where should I start?"

Impa thought a moment, then said, "Go and tell the Maku Tree, the guardian of all Holodrum, what has happened. The tree is located in nearby Horon Village. The tree will tell you what to do."

"What can I do for you, Impa?" asked Link.

"I will be fine once I rest. I will return to the princess as soon as I am able."

With that, Link made Impa comfortable, and set off to find Horon Village. As he walked, he came to a set of wooden pillars. *This must be the entrance to the village,* he thought. As he passed between the pillars, something strange began to happen.

The spring colors began to fade from the world. Trees lost their leaves, and a cold wind began to blow. By the time he had passed between the pillars, snow began to fall and quickly coated the ground. It was winter in Horon Village, but it had been spring moments before!

A girl shivered near the entrance to the village. *This is what losing the Oracle of Seasons has caused. We never know what season it will be from moment to moment!* thought Link.

As Link walked through the frozen village, he saw several buildings and a large gate.

Which building should Link enter?

Bipin and Blossom's home.

Turn to page 60.

The Clock Shop.

Turn to page 8.

The Ring Shop.

Turn to page 42.

Mayor's mansion.

Turn to page 80.

The Village Shop.

Turn to page 9.

Enter the gate.

Turn to page 34.

Leave Horon Village.

Turn to page 72.

22 Gnarled Root Dungeon: *The Maze*

"I'm not sure my Wooden Sword is a match for those blades," Link said. Making a quick decision, he ran past the approaching blade and entered the next room. The red blade was right behind him, but he kept running.

Inside the room, Link saw a round switch on the floor, which he stepped on before the blade could reach him. A chest appeared to the north, and when he opened it, he found a small key inside.

The blade had stopped against the wall, but it began moving as soon as Link tried to leave the room. He was able to stay a few steps ahead of it, and he returned to the other end of the hallway and ran up the stairs.

Link stopped to think. *If I take the mine cart back, there's nothing to explore. I'd better look around a bit here to see if there's a way out,* he thought.

It didn't take long for Link to find what he was looking for. The north wall of the landing he was on had a crack in it. Link placed one of his bombs near the crack, then ran for cover. With a loud *BOOM* the bomb exploded, revealing a passage behind the wall.

When the dust cleared, Link walked through the passage and into the next room. This room was a maze of blocks and blades. The blue blades would only move once,

but the red blades — as Link had found in the previous maze — would follow him. Link found that if he peeked around a corner, the blades would move. When the blue ones moved back to their original spot, he could slip by.

The red blades were more challenging to avoid, but if he teased them into moving and then ducked into alcoves along the way, Link found that they would pass him by as well. As Link neared the end of the maze, he saw a locked door to the north. Avoiding the last spinning blade, Link made a dash for the door, inserted the small key, and ducked inside.

Turn to page 44.

24 Gnarled Root Dungeon:
Blade Battle!

Link drew his sword and stood his ground, waiting for the spinning blade to approach. It moved smoothly down the hall, and just before it reached him, Link started to wonder if he'd made the right choice. Link swung his sword, but the Wooden Sword was no match for the metal blades, which destroyed the sword in seconds. Link turned to run, but he was too late — the deadly blades caught him from behind.

As he fell to the ground, Link felt himself falling and falling, as if the ground wasn't there at all. Deeper into the darkness he fell, until he finally lost consciousness.

Turn to page 77.

Gleeok

Once Link used the Boss Key to unlock the final door, he had to face Gleeok, the guardian of the Essence of Life. Gleeok was a huge, two-headed dragon that spit fireballs from both heads whenever Link got too close. Using the Roc's Cape and his Noble Sword, Link was able to avoid Gleeok's fireball attacks, and he was also able to get close enough to the dragon to cut off one of its heads!

Link was proud of himself, but he soon found out that he wasn't done yet. Gleeok's head was floating around the room and as he watched, it reattached itself to the neck it had been cut from! The dragon was as fierce as he was before, and both heads again spit fireballs at Link.

He tried a few other things, but Link finally decided that to kill Gleeok, he had to hit the other head before the severed one returned to its neck. After several tries and more than one close call, Link was able to strike both heads from the dragon's necks and destroy it.

With the dragon out of the way, it was a short walk to the room where Link found the Essence of Life.

If you have completed the Sword and Shield Dungeon, turn to page 17.

If you have not completed the Sword and Shield Dungeon, turn to page 11.

26 Hero's Cave:
The Path to the Key

Link found himself on a narrow path that was surrounded by a long drop into darkness. Carefully staying on
the path, Link went forward, ready to run at the first sign
of trouble.

He came to a large block of stone on his path.
Remembering the platform he had moved in the other
chamber, Link pushed the block of stone to the north to
get it out of his way and continued along the path.

He didn't encounter any enemies, but he did come to
another dead end. This time, two stone blocks stopped
him from going further. After a few tries, he pushed the
west block south, and the other block to the east, and he
was able to get past them.

Link could see light ahead, and he saw that the path
ended in an entrance to another chamber. As he entered,
he saw several spiders and Gel-like creatures headed his
way.

Moving quickly, Link crossed the room, dodging them
as he ran. When he reached the north end of the room, he
found a small chest.

"It's locked!" he exclaimed. "I wonder where the key is."

As he searched the area, Link saw a small round circle
on the floor nearby. He stepped onto it and heard the lock

on the chest click. He opened the chest and found a small key inside.

Backtracking quickly in order to avoid the creatures in the chamber, Link retraced his steps and returned to the room with the sliding block in the center. This time, he pushed the block and entered the door on the south side of the room.

Turn to page 12.

28 Ghost Battle!

Link knew he couldn't run away, so he immediately jumped down from the ledge and attacked the ghost. Before the ghost could react, he hit her several times with the Noble Sword. To his surprise, the ghost disappeared, promising to return again.

Sheathing his sword, Link looked around for more trouble, but all was quiet again. With the ghost out of the way, he continued exploring. To the west he found a stairway surrounded by heavy weights. Using his power bracelet, he easily pushed them out of the way and followed the stairs down to the first level of the basement.

Turn to page 19.

The Roc's Cape

On the same floor of the dungeon with the huge stat-ues he destroyed, Link found a strange room with a cir-cling platform in the middle. Across the huge room, he could see a chest, but reaching it was going to be tough — there was nothing but darkness surrounding the platforms. If he fell from the platform, he was history!

Link timed a quick jump onto the circling platform and managed to land on it as it spun by. As the platform neared the ledge across the room, he could see that he would have to land exactly on the space in front of the chest. *If I land on those spikes on either side of that space, I'm dead!* thought Link.

Link carefully timed his jump — and made it! He landed in front of the chest and quickly opened it. Inside he found the Roc's Cape. He put it on and left the room. After a few jumps, he realized that the cape allowed him to jump much farther than he could without it.

This was worth the effort, he thought.

Turn to page 10.

The Maku Tree

As Link reentered the village, the seasons changed. The green grass faded and leaves fell from the trees. It was autumn in Horon Village. As Link walked along, he saw children playing in piles of leaves. He passed through the village and neared the gate on the east side of town. Carved on the gate was the message:

ONLY HE WHO SHOWS THE SIGN OF COURAGE MAY ENTER.

Knowing that he'd proven his courage in the Hero's Cave, Link drew his sword and struck the gate. It opened, and he stepped into the forest beyond.

Impa told me to seek out the Maku Tree. It must be somewhere in this forest, thought Link. Soon, Link saw a clearing ahead. A huge tree dominated the clearing. As Link neared it, he knew that it must be the Maku Tree.

As he approached, he could see that the tree was sleeping. Strange images — the tree's dreams — floated nearby. Link didn't know how to wake the tree, so he tried touching one of the dream images with his sword. Immediately, the images vanished and the tree shuddered.

"What? Who . . . ?" The tree's eyes opened and it saw Link. "Who are you? What do you want?" it asked.

Link told the tree who he was, and as Impa had instructed, he told the tree about Din's capture.

The tree sighed. "Guarding the Oracle of Seasons is my duty, but I've failed her. Link, the only way to get her back is to seek out the Temple of Seasons. It used to rest on the

Northern Peak. I sense great evil there now. In order to break the barrier that hides the Temple, you must find the eight Essences of Nature."

The tree yawned hugely. "You will find the first of the Essences in the Gnarled Root Dungeon."

A large key appeared. The tree continued, "Take this key and find the giant root near the lake to the north. This key will allow you to enter the dungeon and find the Essence. The changing seasons have begun to affect me. I'm growing sleepy again, and I'm afraid that . . ."

The tree closed its eyes and fell asleep. Link took the key and left. Back in town, he entered the small shop and used the 30 Rupees he had found to buy a Wooden Shield. He left the shop and headed for the north entrance to the village.

Outside the village, he found Impa again and told her that he had delivered the message to the Maku Tree.

"Good, Link," she said. "Now you must find the eight Essences before it's too late. Go to the north, and you'll find the root the Maku Tree told you about. Be careful!"

Link headed north of the village in search of the gnarled root and the first of the eight Essences of Nature.

Turn to page 51.

32 The Search for the Essences

After Link arrived in Holodrum, he began the search for the other Essences he needed to bring back to the Temple and defeat Onox. His search took him from the Sunken City in the east, to the Spool Swamp far in the west. As he traveled, he frequently returned to Subrosia, gaining mastery of all the seasons through the Rod of Seasons he carried. With the ability to change the seasons as he needed, the Natzu Prairie and the Samasa Desert were reachable, and he searched them for more Essences. The Maku Tree provided support and helped Link as he traveled.

In addition, Link had acquired a new and powerful weapon, the Noble Sword, through a series of trades that had started with the Cuccodex he received from Dr. Left after lighting his torches in Horon Village. In order, he had traded:

- The Cuccodex for the Lon Lon Egg (Malon, north of Horon Village)
- The Lon Lon Egg for the Ghastly Doll (Maple Syrup's apprentice)
- Ghastly Doll for the Iron Pot (Mrs. Ruul's Villa)
- Iron Pot for Lava Soup (Subrosia — Chef's Kitchen)
- Lava Soup for the Goron Vase (Biggoron on top of Goron Mountain)

Link

The Triforce's quest sends Link to the land of Holodrum.

Onox

Onox, General of Darkness, has captured the Oracle of Seasons. Link must defeat Onox and save the Oracle.

Din

Din, the Oracle of Seasons, keeps the seasons in Holodrum in their natural order. When she is kidnapped, only Link can save her and set the seasons right.

Impa

Impa, Zelda's royal nurse, has been sent to Holodrum on a secret mission.

Maku Tree

The mystical Maku Tree is the guardian of the Oracle of Seasons. When the Oracle disappears, the Maku Tree helps Link in his quest to find her.

- Goron Vase for a Fish (Ingo on Mt. Cucco)
- Fish for a Megaphone (Man with a cat in North Horon)
- Megaphone for a Mushroom (Talon, Malon's father inside cave on Mt. Cucco)
- Mushroom for a Wooden Bird (Syrup the Witch in Sunken City)
- Wooden Bird for Engine Grease (Horon Village Clock Shop)
- Engine Grease for Phonograph (East of Horon Village in Windmill)
- Phonograph for the Noble Sword (Lost Woods)

The Noble Sword was more powerful than the Wooden Sword, and it had the ability to shoot a powerful beam of light from its tip, damaging multiple enemies at once. One day, long after his search had begun, the Maku Tree spoke.

"Link, you have found all but two of the Essences you need. You must go to the western coast of Horon Village to seek out the others. You will find them in the Explorer's Crypt, and in the Sword and Shield Dungeon in the Temple Remains. Your quest is nearly at an end, Link — go quickly!"

Link had learned to trust the Maku Tree, and so he set out on the final leg of his journey.

Which dungeon should Link visit first?
The Explorer's Crypt.   **The Sword and Shield Dungeon.**
Turn to page 63.   Turn to page 11.

34 The Gate

As Link explored the village, he found a huge gate in the far northeast corner of Horon. When he tried to enter the gate, he noticed a message carved into the wood of the massive doors.

ONLY HE WHO SHOWS THE SIGN OF COURAGE MAY ENTER.

Link wasn't sure what was behind the gate, but he knew that he didn't have the "Sign of Courage" yet.

I wonder what the "Sign of Courage" is, he thought as he turned away from the gate. Link was certain that the gate and whatever was behind it was important to his quest, and he knew he would have to return here sooner or later.

Turn to page 86.

Battle!

   Link decided to take his chances on the beach, since he wasn't sure where the other tunnel led. As he stepped out onto the beach, he realized that he'd made a bad choice. Several of the Octoroks quickly surrounded him and attacked! With no weapon, Link was forced to retreat. But the Octoroks cut off his escape, even as he tried to get back into the cave. As they knocked him to the ground, Link passed out.

Turn to page 77.

36 Sword and Shield:
Frypolar

As Link explored the dungeon, he found a locked door. Nearby, he came across a stone block with an owl carved on it. He walked up to the block, and when he tried to push it, the owl spoke to him.

"Icy cores make piercing blades," the owl said.

Link had seen these owl stones before, and he realized that this was a clue he would need later. Looking around the room, Link also noticed three stone blocks on the wall with eyes painted on them. He took aim with his Slingshot, and hit all three stones. Immediately, a stairway appeared in the center of the room, and Link took the stairs up.

Upstairs, he battled his way past some soldiers and other creatures to reach a chest with a small key inside. Remembering the locked door, Link ran back down the stairs and unlocked the door with his key.

Inside this large room, Link came face-to-face with a living ball of fire. Frypolar was either pure flame or pure ice, and in either state, he was trouble for Link. As soon as Frypolar saw Link, he started throwing fireballs at him. Link was able to dodge them, but he found out that his sword wasn't going to work against this creature.

Link loaded his Slingshot with Mystery Seeds and hit Frypolar with one. Immediately, Frypolar became icy cold.

On an impulse, Link switched to Ember Seeds and fired one at the cold flame — it worked! Link had found the combination that would destroy Frypolar. Link kept hitting him with seeds, switching between Mystery and Ember Seeds until Frypolar disappeared in a puff of smoke.

As soon as Frypolar was history, the room to the north opened up and Link was able to leave the room.

Which room should Link explore next?
The Torch Room.
Turn to page 62.
The Ice Chamber.
Turn to page 14.

38 Onox's Castle:
Wizzrobes, Soldiers, and Wallmasters

As soon as he entered the room, Link pulled his Slingshot from his pack and loaded it with the magical Pegasus Seeds that had helped him so many times before. Pegasus Seeds would freeze the Wizzrobes in place, allowing Link to attack them while they were frozen.

Link took aim, and froze each of the Wizzrobes with a Pegasus Seed. It was then simple for him to use a powerful spin attack on the helpless Wizzrobes to finish them off. However, his battle was far from over.

In the next room, he was attacked by several Soldiers and Wallmasters. He knew that if the Wallmasters touched him, he would be sent back to the beginning of the castle, so he used the same trick on them. Once the Wallmasters had been frozen by a Pegasus Seed, Link was able to destroy them easily.

Link could tell that he was getting close to Onox's lair. The next chamber appeared too quiet, and as soon as he entered, he knew that he was right. The door slammed shut behind him, and a familiar voice spoke to him.

"So, we meet again, Link. Did you really think I was defeated?"

"Façade!" Link said, unable to keep the surprise from his voice. Link had defeated Façade earlier in his quest and had

not expected to see the creature again. Façade was a powerful being that commanded armies of beetles and created
holes in reality that would destroy Link if he entered them.

Link was surprised, but not frightened. He knew how
to defeat Façade. Before Façade could react, Link threw five
bombs at his face. When the fifth bomb exploded, Façade
was destroyed! Link wasn't sure if he was gone for good,
but at least Façade was out of the way for now.

Turn to page 65.

40 The Temple of Seasons

From the portal through which he had entered Subrosia, Link followed the easternmost set of stairs and kept going south. He saw several Subrosians playing with boomerangs, but he ignored them and turned east to find the Temple. Along the way he passed a dangerous area where lava was spewing from some volcanoes, but he ran past them before any of the hot rocks could hit him.

Link kept heading east, even though the path didn't always go exactly in that direction. Finally, he reached the entrance to the Temple of Seasons. The four Season Spirits spoke to him as he entered, telling him to seek the Rod of Seasons inside the Temple, then come to them in their corner towers.

He walked north into the Temple and found the Rod of Seasons near the center of the building. As soon as Link picked it up, the four Season Spirits spoke to him again, telling him to come to them in their towers located in each corner of the Temple.

As Link searched for the towers, he found that the only tower he could enter was the one to the southeast. Once inside, he was blocked by a river of lava across his path. Across the lava, he could see a small crystal.

I can hit that with my Boomerang, he thought. The Boomerang hit the crystal, which chimed once. A short

bridge appeared across the lava, and Link quickly crossed **41**
over.

Link walked into the next chamber and approached the
statue of the Spirit of Winter. The statue came alive, and
the Spirit charged the Rod of Seasons with the power of
Winter. As soon as Link left the chamber, the Maku Tree
spoke to him, telling him to investigate the forest to the east.

There was no way into the other three Spirit towers
just yet, so Link left the Temple behind and returned to the
portal that led back to the surface world.

Turn to page 32.

42 The Ring Shop

Not far from the center of the village, Link found a building with a large ring on the roof. Curious, he decided to go inside and look around.

There were no customers inside the small shop, but the ring merchant looked at Link with interest. "Come in, come in! How's the weather out there?" Giving Link another look, he added, "Cold, eh? It wasn't a few minutes ago. . . . Ah well, that's life in Horon these days."

Link nodded and looked around the shop. On every table inside glass display cases were rings of every size, color, and shape.

"I'm Vasu, the ring merchant. I see you're admiring my collection," he said. "Of course, none of them are for sale." When Link looked at him strangely, the merchant continued, "You see, I specialize in rare rings that I appraise for those who bring them to me. The ones you see here are waiting for their rightful owners to return and claim them. Of course, for the right price, I could be persuaded to part with them. . . ."

Link smiled. "I'm afraid I'm not in a position to purchase any of them just now. However, I am curious . . . what powers do rings have here?"

Vasu told Link all about rings — how they worked and what they could do. When he was done, he reached beneath the counter and placed a small box on top of it.

"This is a gift for you. It's a Ring Box. Since you can only wear one ring at a time, place any rings you find inside here. While you're wearing one, this box will keep the others safe."

Link thanked him and turned to go.

"Wait! One more thing." Vasu handed Link a small, plain ring. "This is a Friendship Ring. It has no special properties, but keep it as a token of our meeting."

Link put the ring on his finger and thanked the merchant. "Thank you for the information and the ring," he said.

"Don't forget," the merchant shouted as Link left the shop, "I can appraise any rings you find, so come back anytime!"

Link waved, and the door shut, leaving Vasu alone again.

Turn to page 86.

44 Gnarled Root Dungeon:
The Goriya Brothers

As Link entered the next chamber, a mocking voice said, "We cannot allow you to pass. The Goriya Brothers will not be defeated!" The brothers appeared — two menacing Moblins — and each of them was armed with a Boomerang.

Link knew that if he let them get him on the run, he was doomed. Instead, he attacked, intent on taking one of them out to even the odds. He struck with his sword and danced away when a boomerang was thrown at him. Link pressed the attack, pouncing on one of the brothers as it turned away.

Once he had hit one of the brothers five times, they both disappeared in a flash of light, leaving a Health Fairy in their place. Link used the fairy to regain his health, then he noticed a spinning portal in the center of the room.

Link had also seen a door in the west wall of this room, and he decided to explore behind it before entering the portal.

The room beyond the west door had several blade traps along the walls, but since they all moved in straight lines, Link could tease them into moving, then pass as they returned to their original positions. In the center of the room, several stone blocks were arranged into a diamond.

Being careful to avoid the spinning blades, Link made his way around the diamond, looking for a way inside.

On the west side of the diamond, Link noticed some scratch marks beneath the westernmost block. He pushed it north, and it slid out of the way easily. In the center of the diamond, Link found some stairs, and he took them down to the level below.

In the cellar, he found a Seed Satchel full of Ember Seeds. Ember Seeds are very valuable — they burn fiercely and can be used to light torches or burn down trees. Link carefully put the Ember Seeds away, then backtracked until he reached the room with the portal. Then he stepped into the portal.

Turn to page 58.

46 Gnarled Root Dungeon: *Gasha Seed*

Link decided to stay and fight the two Moblins. Although they threw boomerangs at him, he could quickly see that they were easy to dodge as long as he didn't let them back him into a corner. He could also reflect their boomerangs back at them by using his shield.

As soon as a Moblin caught its boomerang, Link had time to run up and hit it with his sword. Once he had finished them both off, Link explored the room. The only interesting thing he found was the stone block in the center of the room.

Let's see if this opens that door in the west wall, he thought, and he pushed the block to the south. Immediately, the west door opened, allowing Link to leave the room.

The next chamber was a maze of large stone blocks that blocked his path. After looking closely at them, Link found that some of them could be moved. After some experimenting, he moved the second block to the north, allowing him to get inside the maze of blocks. He headed for the other end of the maze, and with a few more pushes, he was through the maze and standing on the other side.

A short flight of stairs was all he could see here, so he climbed them. At the top, he found a chest with a Gasha

Seed inside. Gasha Seeds can be planted in soft ground, and when they grow, they can be harvested for items.

Link made his way back through the maze and returned to the chamber with the mine cart. As soon as he jumped into the cart, it rolled back out of the room, returning him to the room full of Gels!

This isn't what I had in mind, he thought. Before the Gels could reach him, Link returned in the mine cart to the room he had just left. The Moblins were back, but since he had already defeated them and knew what was beyond the west door, he chose to take the stairs this time.

Turn to page 82.

48 East Suburbs

Just east of the village, Link was attacked by several Octoroks. Once he had finished them off with some quick sword work, he spotted a tall tower ahead. There was a man on the roof who called down, "You don't have any grease, do you? My windmill needs some."

Link shook his head. "No, sorry, I don't."

To the south of the tower, Link found a hollow log. After walking through it, he came to a beach. As he walked east along the beach, he found the entrance to the Samasa Desert, which was guarded by a Stalfos Pirate. Link didn't have the item the pirate wanted — the Pirate's Bell — so he turned around and walked back through the hollow log.

As Link walked north, he came across a girl with a ribbon in her hair. "Oh . . . um . . . hello," she stammered. "I, uh, I have to get back to somewhere without anyone seeing me, so . . . good-bye!" The girl took off to the north, leaving Link behind.

I think she's keeping a secret. I'd better follow her and see where she goes, thought Link. As he followed her north, Link was careful to keep at least one tree between them at all times so she couldn't see him. She almost saw him when she headed west, because she doubled back suddenly, but Link barely made it into hiding and avoided being seen.

Link followed her west, and saw her disappear into a

patch of plants in a nearby garden. Link was really curious
now, so he chopped down the plants. "Just what I
thought," said Link, "a portal. I'll bet this has something to
do with the Temple of Seasons." Link tucked his sword in
his belt and stepped into the portal.

Turn to page 18.

Sword and Shield:
Medusa Head

Inside the final chamber, Link faced the final boss of the dungeon. The Medusa Head was a massive, blue creature with many serpents growing from her head. One touch from her white fireballs and Link would be turned to stone for a short time. If she managed to hit him with her other attacks during that time, Link would be history!

Instinctively, Link realized that he might be able to stun her momentarily with his Pegasus Seeds — the seeds that would freeze nearly any creature in its tracks. He dodged her attacks until he could get close enough, then he hit her with a Pegasus Seed. It worked! The Medusa Head was frozen for a second or two, long enough for Link to slash at her several times with his sword.

Unfortunately, she shook off the effects of the seed and attacked him again. Link danced away, evading her attacks. He kept up the attack, using the Pegasus Seeds to slow her and his sword to damage her.

The battle was long and slow, but Link was determined not to fail. It wasn't long before the Medusa Head could take no more and disappeared in a flash of light.

In the next chamber, Link found the Changing Seasons Essence on a podium, and he put it in his pack.

If you have completed the Explorer's Crypt dungeon, turn to page 17.

If you have not completed the Explorer's Crypt dungeon, turn to page 63.

The Gnarled Root

After leaving Impa, Link traveled north until he reached a small lake. A long bridge connected the shoreline with a small island in the center of the lake, but the path was blocked by bushes. Link hacked his way through them with his sword and crossed the bridge.

Once on the island, Link found a rock with a keyhole in it and used the key the Maku Tree had given him. As soon as he twisted the key in the keyhole, the ground began to shake. A huge root rose out of the ground, and Link could see a door in the side of it.

This must be the entrance to the dungeon the Maku Tree told me about, he thought. Once the ground stopped shaking, Link stepped through the door and entered the dungeon.

Turn to page 79.

Onox's Castle: *Entry*

Before Link could enter Onox's Castle, he had to get by the two Fire Cats guarding the entrance. Using the Roc's Cape and the Noble Sword, he was able to run past the two guardians and slip into the castle before they could catch him.

Once he was inside the castle, Link found himself in a long hallway with doors to the left and right. Both doors looked the same, so he entered the one on the left. Immediately, the door slammed shut, trapping him inside! As Link tried to pry the door open, the floor began to shake, and loose floor tiles began to fly at him.

Link made his way to the corner of the room, swatting flying tiles with his sword. As he battled toward the corner, he came across a health fairy who restored his health. Link stood in the corner and hit any tiles that got too close until they had all been destroyed. As soon as the tiles were gone, the door opened again.

Back in the hall, Link walked north. In the second room ahead, he was ambushed. Several Wizzrobes were waiting for him, and they quickly attacked!

How should Link fight the Wizzrobes?
Use the Noble Sword.
Turn to page 64.
Use his Slingshot.
Turn to page 38.

Gnarled Root Dungeon: 53
The Red Blade

The mine cart took Link east, past the Gel room. Several spiders attacked while he was in the cart, but he was able to hit them with his sword as he rolled along. He noticed a chest beside the tracks, but the cart kept going. *I'll have to come back for that,* he thought.

Finally, the mine cart rolled to a stop and Link jumped out. Remembering the chest he had seen along the tracks, Link ran back to it and found that it contained some bombs.

"These will be useful if I have to blast a hole in a wall," said Link as he tucked them into his pack.

Link returned to the room where the mine cart was sitting and ran up the stairs nearby. He turned the corner at the top and went down another set of stairs into a block-lined hallway. As he turned the first corner in the hallway, a spinning red blade came toward him from a side passage.

What should Link do?
Destroy the blade.
Turn to page 24.
Run past the blade.
Turn to page 22.

Hero's Cave: *The Trap*

Link decided to take his chances exploring the cave, since he didn't think he could fight the Octoroks outside or get away from them.

If I see any enemies in here, or if something attacks me, I'll have to get away instead of stopping to fight, he thought. He could hear noises around him as he explored the first chamber, so he ran quickly into the next room.

As soon as he entered the room, the doors on the north and south sides closed, trapping him inside!

Link noticed a small platform in the center of the room. He didn't see anything remarkable about it, but as he looked closely he could see that there were scratch marks on the floor around the platform.

Hoping he was doing the right thing, Link put his shoulder against the side of the platform and pushed it. The platform slowly slid across the floor, and suddenly, the doors to the room opened again!

Which door should Link choose?
North.
Turn to page 26.
South.
Turn to page 76.

56 The Trading Game: *Part 1*

Link decided to take the Cuccodex to Malon, so he left Horon Village and headed north. He found Malon in her house, surrounded by cuccos. "Please, can you help me?" she asked. Link reached into his pack and handed her the Cuccodex. "This is just what I needed!" Malon said. "Now I can figure out how to raise these birds the way my father did."

Malon reached into her apron and handed a small egg to Link. "This is a Lon Lon Egg. It's a beauty item that's popular with most girls. You might find a use for it in your travels."

Looking oddly at the egg, Link shrugged and put it in his pack. Malon thanked him again, and Link waved to her as he headed back to the village.

I'm not sure what kind of trade that was, thought Link. *I can't use either of those things — the book or the egg.*

Just then, a shadow appeared on the ground, and Link barely had time to brace himself before he was knocked down. Lying on the ground near him was a girl who had been flying on a broom.

"Hey!" she shouted as she straightened her hat. "Watch where you're going! I'm Maple Syrup, the Witch's apprentice, and you'd better have a good explanation for getting in my way!"

Link was dusting himself off. As he picked up his pack, **57** the Lon Lon Egg fell out onto the ground.

"Oh!" cried Maple. "You've got a Lon Lon Egg." Her voice changed to a nicer tone and she helped Link to his feet. "I'd really like to have that egg." She reached into her pocket and held out a very odd-looking doll. "Trade me the Lon Lon Egg for this Ghastly Doll, and we'll just forget about our little accident."

Link didn't have any reason not to trade, so he took the Ghastly Doll and dropped it into his pack and then gave her the egg. "Thanks," said Maple. "I hope we don't run into each other again!" With that, she flew off on her broom.

Shaking his head, Link kept walking south and headed for the southeast corner of Horon Village, where he had burned the sapling to reveal a new area to explore.

•

Turn to page 48.

58 Gnarled Root Dungeon: *Means to an End*

After stepping through the portal, Link found himself near the mine cart in the Gel room. Using his spinning attack, he quickly destroyed all the Gels in the room, then he approached the locked door in the west wall.

There were two unlit torches, one on either side of the door. Link placed an Ember Seed on each torch, and as soon as they were lit, the door magically opened. Three boomerang-tossing Moblins waited to ambush Link in the next room. Link tracked each of them down and hit each of them twice to get rid of them.

As soon as all the Moblins were gone, a magic chest appeared in the center of the room. Inside, Link found the Boss Key. There was nothing else in the room, so Link backtracked to the room with the four stone blocks inside. He remembered to push the northeast block to open the doors, and then he entered the east door.

Once again, he had to fight off the four Stalfos inside the room. Once they were gone, he aproached the door on the north side of the room. There were two unlit torches on either side of the door, so he placed an Ember Seed on each of them to open the door.

Beyond the door was another block maze, but this one was very different. As soon as Link entered, Wallmasters began to appear. Wallmasters were ghostly blue hands that would send Link back to the beginning of the dungeon if they touched him. Link had to hit each of them with his sword several times to get them out of his path as he made his way through the maze.

On the left side of the room, Link found a chest with a ring inside. *I'll have to get this appraised by the jeweler in Horon Village*, he thought as he tucked it into his pack. Once he had made his way through the maze, Link faced a locked door. Link readied his sword and shield, and used the Boss Key to open the door.

Turn to page 88.

60 Bipin and Blossom's Home

Link noticed a small house near the center of the village. He wasn't sure where to find the Maku Tree, so he knocked on the door to get directions.

"Hello," said the woman who answered the door. "Please, come in out of the cold!"

Link entered the warm house. Inside, he noticed a man bending over a cradle in the corner.

"Welcome, stranger," the man said. "It's too cold to be outside right now. Why don't you come in and warm yourself by the fire?" The man lifted a tiny bundle from the crib, and Link could see a baby's face peeking out.

Link introduced himself and found out that their names were Bipin and Blossom. When he asked what the baby's name was, the parents looked at each other, then sheepishly shrugged at Link.

"We haven't named him yet," Blossom said. "Finding the right name is hard!"

"Perhaps . . . perhaps you can help us think of a name for him?" asked Bipin hopefully.

Link thought for a moment and said, "Why don't you name him Bipsom, after both of you?"

The parents smiled. "That's a wonderful idea, Link! Bipsom he shall be!"

Link felt like he was intruding, so he declined their offer to spend the night. Bipin showed him to the door, patting him on the back. "Thanks for your help with Bipsom's name, Link. We'll never forget you — nor shall he!"

With that, Link left the house and stepped out into the cold.

Turn to page 86.

62 Sword and Shield:
The Torch Room

After leaving the chamber where he had defeated Frypolar, Link entered a large room with a platform in the middle. On this platform, Link found an unlit torch. Along both walls, he could see other platforms with unlit torches. There were three unlit torches on each side of the room, plus the one in the middle.

Link lit the center torch with an Ember Seed, then used his Slingshot to sling Ember Seeds at the others. He had to try this several times, because it had to be done so that all the torches were lit at the same time. Once they were all lit together, a set of stairs appeared near the center torch, allowing Link to climb up.

Turn to page 73.

The Explorer's Crypt

On the western coast of Horon Village, Link found an ancient graveyard on the west side of the pirate ship anchored nearby. Inside, he found a set of stairs that led into the Explorer's Crypt.

The Crypt was a dark and mysterious place, and Link could tell instantly that there was a curse laid upon its very walls. As he walked through the first few chambers of the Crypt, several Stalfos attacked him. After he took care of them, he noticed that if he walked through the room in different directions, the exits would take him to different rooms. He decided to handle all the rooms the same way — he would walk in a clockwise direction each time. That way his choices would all be the same.

He came to a ledge above a dark room. Since he couldn't see anything, he loaded the Slingshot he'd found during his travels with Ember Seeds and shot the two torches on the ledge.

Immediately, a horrible ghost appeared from a nearby gravestone.

What should Link do?
Fight the ghost.
Turn to page 28.
Run away.
Turn to page 71.

64 Onox's Castle: *Defeat!*

Link waded into battle with the Wizzrobes, using the Noble Sword's light beam to attack. Things were going well for a few minutes, but the Wizzrobes were too fast. One of them got behind Link while he was busy fighting the others, and with one quick strike, it was over. Link fell to the floor, unconscious.

As he blacked out, Link could hear Onox laughing, and the sound followed him down into the darkness.

Turn to page 77.

The Fall of Onox

Link entered the next chamber and found himself in Onox's lair. As soon as he entered, Onox appeared and the battle began.

Onox's armor was strong, and Link quickly found that the only thing that could damage it was his spin attack. When Onox swung his mace over his head, Link could dart in and use the spin attack to damage the powerful general. Using Pegasus Seeds helped as well, giving Link time to dodge Onox's attacks. Link landed seven blows on Onox, and the general called out, "Din, come to me."

The helpless Din, imprisoned in a blue, jewel-shaped prison, spun into the room. The prison crackled with electricity, and Link knew that if it touched him he would be seriously hurt.

The Maku Tree spoke to Link as Din approached. "Use the Rod of Seasons, Link! The Rod will keep the prison from hurting you!" Link didn't hesitate. He drew the Rod of Seasons from his pack and used it to keep Din away from him. Keeping an eye on Din's deadly prison, Link then continued his attack on Onox.

Onox tried summoning rocks to fall on Link, as well as small tornadoes, but Link avoided them all. Link was able to hit Onox four times without touching Din's prison. On the fourth blow, Onox disappeared and the floor began to

66 shake. A huge hole appeared in the floor, and Link fell through!

The chamber below was dark, but just as Link began looking for a way out, a sinister voice spoke.

"Onox was but a shadow of my true self," it said. "It is certain that you will die, Link, but before you do, look upon my true form and be afraid." From out of the shadows, a giant dragon appeared. "I am the Dark Dragon, and your quest is at an end, Hero of Hyrule!"

Link backed away, looking for an opening to attack. He could tell that the Dark Dragon's scales were too tough for his sword, or any of his other weapons. With a roar, the Dark Dragon's huge claw swept along the ground, barely missing Link.

Out of desperation, Link leaped on top of the dragon's claw. With a lunge, he swung his sword at the creature's face, hitting the red gem in its forehead. The creature swayed as Link leaped to the other claw. *I'll bet that it won't shoot fire at me while I'm on its claws,* thought Link.

The dragon tried to shake Link from its claws, but each time one of its claws got close to his face, Link used a spin attack to hit the gem. The fourth time Link managed to do this, the Dark Dragon bellowed in pain.

"No! It's too late. My orders were to capture Din and deliver the destructive power of a seasonless land to Twinrova. Now, as the Flame of Destruction, that power is

set to devour the land. A-ha-ha — you have beaten me, Link, but you have lost after all!"

With that, the Dark Dragon disappeared. Din's prison glowed brightly and shattered, freeing her. She ran to Link, and they held each other tightly as Onox's castle began to fall apart.

"Quickly," she said, "we must leave this place!" The pair dodged falling rocks and made their way out of the castle and back across the walkway to safety.

As soon as they were safe, Link asked Din about the Dark Dragon's final words.

"What did it mean . . . who is Twinrova? I met them when I was entering the castle," said Link.

"I don't know, Link," said Din. "For now, I am happy that you came for me." With a sly look, Din took Link's hand. "Remember, you still owe me a dance!" Link smiled, and the two began the trip back to Horon Village, where Impa was waiting to take Din to Zelda.

Link was glad Din was safe, but he felt uneasy. *I'm sure this isn't over yet*, he thought. Unfortunately, he was right.

The End

Be sure to continue Link's adventure by reading *The Legend of Zelda®: Oracle of Ages™*!

68 Gnarled Root Dungeon: *All Aboard!*

As soon as he entered the east room, Link was attacked by four skeletal warriors — Stalfos. By staying on the move, Link was able to defeat them with his sword. As soon as the Stalfos were gone, a key appeared in the center of the room.

Link picked up the key and returned to the room with the four stone blocks, and tried the key in the lock of the west door. It was a perfect fit, and the locked door opened at once. Link stepped through the door into the next chamber.

Four more Stalfos were waiting to ambush Link in this room, but he knew what to do. Once the Stalfos were gone, a magic chest appeared in the center of the room. Link opened the chest and found a map to the dungeon inside!

This map will make it much easier to find the first Essence, thought Link.

The north door to the chamber was also open, so Link headed north to explore the next part of the dungeon.

There were no Stalfos in the next room, but several small Gels began oozing their way toward Link. "If those small Gels catch me, I won't be able to fight off the larger ones with my sword." Link used a spinning attack to de-

stroy the small Gels before they could reach him, and quickly finished off the larger Gels, too.

At the north end of the room, Link discovered a mine cart sitting on rails that disappeared under the wall ahead. He knew that he couldn't explore the rooms behind him further, so without looking back, Link jumped into the mine car, which rolled across the rails and was on a collision course with the wall! At the last instant, as Link braced himself to hit the wall, the wall disappeared, and the mine car rolled through the gap.

Turn to page 83.

70 Tricks and Traps

The Roc's Cape that Link found earlier proved to be very valuable. When he came across floors that would crack and begin to break as soon as he landed on them, he was able to jump to another floor tile before the floor collapsed. The deeper he went into the Crypt, the more often this happened.

Link also had to use the Magnetic Gloves he had found in another dungeon several times. The gloves pulled him toward magnets, or pushed him away if he changed their polarity. Using this trick, Link was able to cross huge pits and reach areas that the Roc's Cape alone couldn't help him reach.

After a very difficult place where there was hardly any floor for him to stand on, Link had to battle a room full of Stalfos. The pesky skeletons nearly did him in, but he managed to defeat them and open the chest that appeared in the room. Inside, he found the Boss Key. The Boss Key would unlock the final door that led to the master of this dungeon — Gleeok.

Turn to page 25.

Retreat!

Link didn't hesitate — as soon as he saw the ghost, he turned and ran from the room. Unfortunately, the ghost was much faster than he was, and it blocked his exit. Before Link could use his sword, he was knocked unconscious, and he fell to the dungeon floor.

Turn to page 77.

72 Outside Horon Village

Rather than explore the village, Link decided to explore the countryside nearby for clues to help him find Din.

North of the village, Link quickly ran into trouble. Several creatures spotted him, and he was forced to retreat. With no weapon, he realized that he shouldn't be wandering around in the wilderness.

I'd better go back to the village, and maybe later I'll be ready to explore here, he thought. With that, Link returned to Horon Village.

Which building should Link enter?
Bipin and Blossom's home.
Turn to page 60.
The Clock Shop.
Turn to page 8.
The Ring Shop.
Turn to page 42.
Mayor's mansion.
Turn to page 80.
The Village Shop.
Turn to page 9.
Enter the gate.
Turn to page 34.

Sword and Shield:
The Magic Ice

Link traveled deeper into the dungeon, battling his way through the various chambers and destroying the creatures in his path. Along the way, he found the Boss Key that would let him face the final boss of this dungeon. Eventually, he came to an icy chamber with an owl stone inside. When he used a Mystery Seed on the owl stone, it told him to melt all the magical ice.

He could see some blue ice crystals. *These must be what the owl stone was talking about,* thought Link. He used his Power Bracelet to lift one of the ice crystals and walked into the room to the south. There was a lava pit there, so Link tossed the ice crystal into the lava.

The ice cooled the lava, giving Link a surface he could use to walk across. He found a small key in the lava chamber once he crossed over the cooled walkway, and then he returned to the owl stone chamber.

Link found a crack in the wall and used a bomb to break through it. With another ice crystal in hand, he explored the chamber beyond the hole in the wall. He used the mine cart he found to carry the ice to the end of the line. There he dropped the magic ice into the last lava pit he could find, and took the ten bombs from the chest across the lava.

74 Before entering the final chamber to the north, Link broke open the vases near the wall and used the health fairies inside to replenish his health. Once he was ready, Link used the Boss Key to open the door ahead and enter the final chamber of the dungeon.

Turn to page 50.

The Subrosian Dance Hall

Link made his way down the west stairs. Near the lava baths, he found a sign that pointed to the dance hall. Near the sign, he came across a Subrosian who told him that if he wanted a Boomerang, he should go to the dance hall.

He found the dance hall to the south and once inside the hall, Link was asked to join in a Subrosian ritual dance. The instructor spoke to Link before the dance started.

"You must perform the steps in the right order. Good dancers will get a prize!"

Link wasn't sure about the dance, but he stepped onto the floor. Although it took him several tries, he eventually learned the dance well enough to earn the instructor's praise (or at least well enough that she was ready to get rid of him).

"Well done!" she said. "Take this Boomerang as your reward for learning our dance so well."

Link thanked the instructor, then headed for the portal landing again.

Turn to page 40.

76 Hero's Cave: Dead End!

Link entered the door on the south side of the chamber and found himself in a large, square room with a locked door on the east wall. To make matters worse, there were four spiders in the room, and they had already spotted him.

Dodging the spiders, Link quickly explored the room. There was no key to be found, but he did see four square platforms. He experimented by pushing them, but nothing happened.

"The key must be in another chamber," he said, and left the room through the north doorway. He was once more in the chamber with the sliding block, but this time, he pushed the block and entered the door on the north side of the room.

Turn to page 26.

End of the Road

Link woke up and found himself on the floor in front of the Triforce. "I'm back in Hyrule!" he exclaimed. He remembered his quest to help Din, but now he knew that he had failed. *What will I tell Zelda?* he thought. With a heavy heart, Link turned from the Triforce and left the room, wishing that he had another chance to rescue Din and defeat Onox.

The End

Sorry, but you've reached the worst possible ending of this story. Care to try again?

78 Gnarled Root Dungeon:
Lighten up!

Link decided to try the north door, and so he set off in that direction. Once inside the next room, he found a strange man. Link approached the man, and when he was close enough, the man spoke to him.

"Light is the key. You must return light to unlit torches."

Link wasn't sure what he meant, but he thanked the man. The man simply repeated his message and looked meaningfully at Link. Bored with the conversation, Link decided to return to the room to the south.

"I guess I'll try the room to the east," he said once he had returned to the room with the four stone blocks. He pushed the northeast block, then entered the east door.

Turn to page 68.

Gnarled Root Dungeon:
Entry

Once inside the dungeon, Link knew he had to explore carefully — there was no telling what creatures lived in a place like this, or what traps might lurk in the darkness. The first room of the dungeon was creepy — watching eyes peered at him from platforms scattered around the room. Link quickly ran past them into the next room.

As soon as he entered the room, all the doors slammed shut. He was trapped! Link searched the room and found four stone blocks. Remembering the sliding block in the Hero's Cave, Link guessed that one of these blocks would unlock the doors. After a few tries, he found that if he pushed the northeast block in any direction, the doors would unlock.

Now Link had a choice — there were two open doors, north and east. The door to the west was locked.

Which door should Link enter?
North.
Turn to page 78.
East.
Turn to page 68.

80 The Mayor's Mansion

Located on a hill on the northeast side of the village Link saw a large mansion.

Someone important must live here, he thought. He knocked on the front door, and it immediately opened.

Inside, Link found Ruul, the mayor of Horon. The mayor was busy placing plants in small pots, but he looked up when Link walked in.

"You must be Link. Din told me about you." A sad look crossed Ruul's face. "Of course, that was before she was taken."

Link nodded grimly. "I'm going to bring her back. Is there anything you can tell me that might help?"

"I'm afraid not, Link. For the most part, I'm a simple gardener." Ruul gestured at the plants surrounding him. "Being the mayor isn't a full-time job, so I keep busy by using my green thumb."

Reaching into his pocket, he handed Link a small seed. "This might help you, though. It's a Gasha Seed. I know it doesn't look like much, but if you plant it in the ground, it will reward you by providing a special item when it grows. Maybe that will help you in your quest to rescue Din."

Link thanked the mayor, who told him more about the seed. It seemed that the seed would only grow in certain types of soil, and Ruul made sure Link knew how to find the right place to grow the seed.

Finally, Link turned to go. "Thank you again for the seed, Mayor. I'll find Din and bring her back. I promise."

"Good luck, Link!" shouted the mayor, and he watched Link as he left. "You'll need all the luck you can get!" he added after Link was gone.

Turn to page 86.

82 Gnarled Root Dungeon: *Quick Switch*

Link ran up the stairs on the right. At the top of the stairs, he was attacked by some spiders, but he quickly destroyed them with his sword and kept running east.

He spotted a switch sticking out of the floor ahead, and as he got closer to it, he could see that it was on a ledge over the mine cart tracks. Link hit the switch once with his sword, and he saw the mine cart tracks shift. *I think that the mine cart will take me somewhere else now,* he thought.

Before he headed back to the cart, Link kept going east. He had to fight more spiders, but he was rewarded by finding a chest with a Compass inside. A Compass was a very useful item — it would help Link find the boss room, keys, and chests on his Dungeon Map.

Tucking the Compass in his pocket, Link ran back to the west and down the stairs. The Moblins in the room saw him, but before they could attack, Link jumped into the mine cart and sped away down the tracks.

Turn to page 53.

Gnarled Root Dungeon:
Decision

Link rode the mine cart down the tracks, swinging his sword to fight off the spiders that swarmed the tracks. Finally, he could see light at the end of the tracks, and the train emerged into another room. When the mine cart stopped, Link jumped out.

He found himself in a large room with a closed door in the west wall and a stone block in the center of the room. He could also see a short flight of stairs on his right. Unfortunately, he wasn't alone — two large Moblins were headed his way! As they approached, each of them threw a large boomerang at Link.

Link had a choice. He could stay and fight the Moblins, or run up the stairs to get away.

What should Link do?
Stay and fight.
Turn to page 46.
Run up the stairs.
Turn to page 82.

84 Horon Village

It was winter in Horon Village again. *These season changes are hard to get used to,* thought Link. Since he had been here before, Link knew that he didn't need to visit every building, so he strolled around the village looking for anything interesting.

His first stop was the Ring Shop, where he got the ring that he'd found in the Gnarled Root Dungeon appraised. It was a Discovery Ring, and when he wore it, he'd be able to find fertile soil for Gasha Seeds to grow in. When Gasha Seeds mature, they become Gasha Nuts and contain valuable items or Rupees, so this was a good ring to have.

Behind the Ring Shop, Link climbed the short flight of stairs and used an Ember Seed to burn down a sapling so he could reach the heart piece behind it.

On the south side of the village, Link found a strange tree that grew Ember Seeds. He used his sword to knock them down and put them in his pack. Nearby, to the east, he entered a small dark hut.

Dr. Left, who lived in the hut, asked if Link could bring him some light. Link used an Ember Seed to light the torch nearby, and Dr. Left was extremely grateful.

"Here, take this Cuccodex. . . . You never know who might find it useful. Malon, who lives north of town, raises cuccos . . . or at least, her father did. Maybe she can use it." While he was talking, Link noticed a crack in the wall.

Dr. Left, who was busy reading, didn't seem to mind when Link placed a bomb near it and blew a hole in the wall. This allowed Link to enter a small outdoor courtyard. Across an icy pond, Link was able to reach a chest with some Rupees inside.

Just south of Dr. Left's hut, Link burned one of three saplings to reveal an underground chamber. A wise man, meditating inside, gave him 100 Rupees to go away, so Link left and returned to the surface.

In the southeast corner of the village, Link talked to a boy playing with his dog. "You can burn these saplings," he said, pointing to the three trees nearby. "But be careful with the fire!"

Link could see that there was an open area to the east behind the three saplings, so he burned one down. *This looks like a good place to search for the item the Maku Tree mentioned,* thought Link.

What should Link do?
Search the area to the east.
Turn to page 48.
Take the Cuccodex to Malon.
Turn to page 56.

86 The Hero's Cave

Link meant to explore the rest of the village, but just then he noticed a small boy playing in the snow. When Link asked him about the Maku Tree, the boy said, "The Maku Tree is beyond the gates at the northeast end of town, but everyone knows that the gates will only open for one of great courage. Find the Hero's Cave near the beach — you can prove your courage there."

Link thanked the boy and continued walking. He soon found another set of pillars marking the west edge of the village. When he stepped through the pillars, he immediately found himself beneath a clear blue sky. Green grass covered the hillside, and birds sang in the trees. It was spring again!

Taking off his cloak, Link followed the path down the hill and reached the beach. He searched the area and came across several strange creatures. Link dodged just in time as one of the creatures — an Octorok — attacked! With no weapon, Link knew he couldn't fight it, so he ran from the creature and the others like it he saw on the beach.

Just in time, Link found the opening to a cave and ducked inside. The cave was small, but he could see another opening that led deeper underground. Link wasn't sure what to do — he didn't want to face the creatures outside without a weapon, but he didn't know where the other tunnel went.

What should Link do?
Go back to the beach and try to outrun the Octoroks.
Turn to page 35.
Head deeper into the cave.
Turn to page 54.

88 Gnarled Root Dungeon: *Aquamentus*

As soon as Link entered the massive room, Aquamentus, the guardian of the Essence of Nature, attacked. Aquamentus was a huge, horned beast that breathed fireballs and defended its territory with brutal charging attacks.

Link stood his ground against the beast's first charge, blocking it with his shield. Aquamentus's fireball attacks couldn't be blocked, though, and Link was slightly injured by one of them.

Learning from his mistake, Link used his shield to block Aquamentus's charges, and he dodged the fireball attacks. As soon as he had an opening, Link hit the beast with his sword. It had no effect! Aquamentus attacked again, and Link swung wildly, hitting the creature on its horn.

Aquamentus bellowed in pain. "That's it!" cried Link. "That horn is its weak spot!" Link waded in, sword swinging, and attacked Aquamentus's horn. Making sure he was ready for the beast's counterattacks, Link kept fighting.

After twenty blows to Aquamentus's horn, the beast suddenly began to shake. With a huge explosion, it disappeared. Aquamentus had been defeated!

Link entered the door Aquamentus had been guarding, and found the Essence of Nature. This Essence would al-

low the Gasha Seeds Link planted to grow, allowing him to harvest them for items later. With his quest in the dungeon complete, Link turned and left the dungeon to find the other seven Essences.

Once outside the dungeon, the Maku Tree spoke to Link. "There is an item that will help you greatly in your quest. Look for it in the hidden land where the Temple of Seasons has gone."

Link didn't know where the hidden land was, so he had to decide where to go next. He could return to Horon Village, or seek out the item the Maku Tree had spoken about in the land nearby.

What should Link do?
Return to Horon Village.
Turn to page 84.
Search for the item.
Turn to page 94.

90 Hero's Cave: *Secret Chamber*

Link dropped through the hole and found himself in a well-lit chamber. He discovered a chest along one wall and opened it to find that it was full of Rupees.

Thirty Rupees! Now I should be able to buy some supplies, he thought.

The room he was in was actually a ledge above the first chamber of the cave, so he jumped down. With his new weapon, Link decided to explore the cave in search of more Rupees (or other items).

He went into the chamber with the sliding platform and pushed it to enter the room to the south.

Link quickly killed all the spiders in the room and looked closely at the four platforms. There were scratch marks on the floor just south of the northwest block, so he put his shoulder against it and pushed it south.

A secret door in the floor of the room opened, revealing a staircase. Link climbed down the stairs and into a secret chamber.

Inside, he found a ledge with a Gasha Seed on it. *This was well worth the effort,* he thought, and he left the chamber.

Satisfied that he had explored the cave thoroughly, Link left the cave and returned to Horon Village.

Turn to page 30.

Sword and Shield Dungeon:
Entry

Link cautiously entered the dungeon and found himself in a long hallway that led north. In the first section of the hallway, there was a small room to the east. Link entered it and saw a strange stone block with an eye on it across the room. A pit kept Link from reaching the block, so he pulled out his Slingshot and loaded it with seeds. He tried all the seeds he had, but when he hit the block with a Mystery Seed, a small key dropped onto the floor on his side of the pit.

He grabbed the key and left the room, continuing north. Link found another key when he defeated a Hardhat Beetle in another of the rooms along the hallway. From this room, he headed east, deeper into the dungeon.

In a small chamber full of Keese, Link found some stairs that led down into the basement. He avoided the Wallmaster in the room and took the stairs down to the dungeon below.

Turn to page 16.

92 Onox's Castle

The Maku Tree told Link where to find Onox. Onox's Castle was hidden far to the north in the Tarm Ruins, and Link might never have found it without the Tree's help. When Link reached the area near the Temple Remains, he walked to the west to enter the Northern Peak. The castle was located to the north.

As soon as Link stepped onto the walkway of the castle, he held the Maku Seed high above his head and called out in a clear voice, "Essences of Nature, hear me! Break the spell and let me pass!" There was a loud noise like the rushing of many winds, and the Maku Seed glowed brightly. As the Maku Seed began to disappear, a change came over Onox's Castle — the spell that had protected it was gone!

As Link began walking toward the castle, two creatures appeared.

"Are you shocked?" they asked at the same time. "We are Twinrova — Onox is just a pawn in this game. No matter what happens in your battle with Onox, the Evil King will still return to spread darkness across the land. Your quest is hopeless, Hero of Hyrule!" With that, Twinrova disappeared, leaving Link to wonder if their claim was true.

"No matter what, I still have to defeat Onox to free Din," said Link, and he crossed the walkway to reach the castle.

Turn to page 52.

Outside Horon Village

Link decided that he should search the area outside Horon Village for the item the Maku Tree mentioned. Near the bridge that led to the Gnarled Root, Link noticed something odd about one of the trees. The tree nearest the water was younger than the others. Using an Ember Seed, Link burned it down to reveal a secret passage.

Below, he found a wise man. "Shhh! Don't tell!" the wise man pleaded. "Here, take these one hundred Rupees and keep quiet — I'm meditating!" Link left quickly, pocketing the Rupees. Once he was back aboveground, Link headed east.

He was immediately attacked by a swarm of Octoroks. It was a fierce battle, but Link was able to dodge their attacks and get past them. His path was blocked to the east, but a narrow path to the north led to a small house.

The house was overrun with cuccos, and inside the house, he found Malon, a young lady with a problem. "You see, my father knows all about these birds, but he's gone and I don't have a clue what to do for them. Can you help?"

"I don't know anything about them either," Link said, "but I'll keep my eyes open for anything that might help you."

Link left the house and thought about his next move. "It looks like I'll have to go back to Horon Village — there's nowhere else to go out here." With that, Link trudged back to the south and entered the village again.

Turn to page 84.

96

Look out for the next book in the Game Boy® Color series:

The Legend of Zelda: Oracle of Ages

Join Link on his latest travels around a vast underworld.